This famous story was first published in 1818, but the monster that Frankenstein created is as frightening as ever. Sometimes, though, a sneaking sympathy can creep in for the life it has to lead...

First edition

LADYBIRD HORROR CLASSICS

FRANKENSTEIN

by Mary Shelley

retold in simple language
by Raymond Sibley
illustrated by Jon Davis

Ladybird Books Loughborough

Victor Frankenstein was born in 1770. He was his parents' first child, and they treated him with such tenderness and love that his childhood was very happy. This was not surprising for the Frankensteins were good people, generous and kind to the poor. They had many friends in Geneva where they lived.

When he was five, Victor received an unusual gift. One morning, when he was on holiday in Milan with his parents, his mother called to him.

'I have a pretty present for you, Victor.'

Standing there with her was a beautiful, golden-haired little girl of about his own age.

'This is Elizabeth,' said his mother.

From the very first, Victor looked upon Elizabeth as his own, and promised to love and look after her always. His mother told him later that the girl was of good family but that her parents were dead. As she had no one left, she was coming to live with them. The two children grew up together. Elizabeth calm and soft-voiced; Victor a little uncertain of temper sometimes, but they were happy, carefree and affectionate with one another.

When Victor was seven his brother Ernest was born, and shortly afterwards the family moved for a while to their country house at Belrive. This second home was on the eastern shore of the lake, a short distance from the city gates of Geneva.

'I am so pleased,' Victor said to Elizabeth, 'for I don't like the crowds in Geneva; but I do like being alone in the quiet of Belrive.'

Apart from Elizabeth, his only friend was Henry Cherval, the son of a merchant. But there was something different in Victor that he told nobody about, not even Elizabeth and Henry.

For, while Elizabeth loved the natural beauty of the Swiss countryside and Henry thrilled to tales of knights in armour, action and adventure, Victor's interest was in the darker side of nature. He thought deeply about the secrets and mysteries of life and death.

It so filled his mind that he spent every minute he could alone reading books on how life could be created and what happened to people's spirits after they had died. Soon he turned to the study of ghosts and devils. A year or so later his second brother William was born, by which time Victor had become fascinated by his subject.

One evening, when he was about fifteen, he saw something which made a great impression on him. A thunderstorm had formed over the Jura

mountains, and broke violently over the house and lake. One flash of lightning shattered a tree close by the house. Victor never forgot the picture of the blasted stump, nor the power of electricity.

He reached seventeen and was ready to begin his studies at the university of Ingolstadt when he suffered a great loss. His mother died of scarlet fever. On her death bed she joined his hands with those of Elizabeth. 'My children,' she said, 'it has always been my hope that one day you two will marry each other. Elizabeth my love, be a mother to little William and Ernest.' She died calmly.

After a few weeks Victor prepared to make the long and tiring coach journey to the university. Sadly he said goodbye to his father, Elizabeth, his two young brothers, and Henry Cherval.

'Please write often,' said Elizabeth tearfully.

*   *   *

After a few days at the university, Frankenstein decided that he would spend his time exploring unknown powers and the deep mystery of the creation of life. He was so excited that he found it difficult to sleep. Nothing else entered his mind. He forgot Elizabeth, his father, his friend Henry and his brothers. For two years he did not think of them, so deep was he in his experiments. To begin with, he studied the medicine of life. He visited churchyards and burial chambers to observe the effect of death on the body. Always his mind went back to the thunderstorm and the violent force of electricity. Could it create as well as destroy? After many months of experiment he discovered how to use that force to put life into something dead. He wondered how he should use the power he had gained. He decided to make a man!

So in a lonely room at the top of his lodgings he began his work. He collected pieces from slaughter houses, doctors' laboratories, churchyards, and any place where the dead could be found. That first year had a beautiful summer but Victor did not notice; he could not tear himself from what he was making in the upper room. Winter and spring followed but he did not heed them. He began to look haggard; his nerves were on edge. He lost weight but still worked on.

One dreary November night he succeeded in giving a spark of life to his creation. By the light of a flickering candle he saw a limb twitch. It breathed and one eye jerked open. Victor looked down at the thing he had created. The skin was yellow and tightly stretched over the body. In size the creature was huge but the eyes, under the dark hair, were watery. The flesh on the face was shrivelled and the lips straight and blackish.

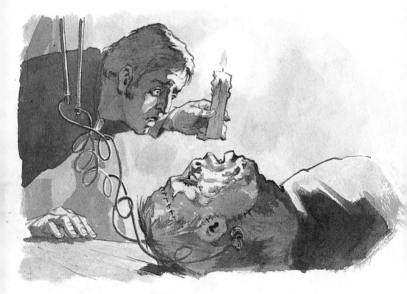

Now that he had succeeded, Frankenstein felt nothing but disgust. Once he had seen it, the horror became too much for him. He could not bear to look at the monster.

He rushed from the room in terror. Inside his own bedroom he tried to calm himself. He lay on his bed fully clothed but slept fitfully for he had dreadful nightmares, of worms and his dead mother. Suddenly he awoke. His forehead was damp with sweat and his teeth chattered.

There at the foot of the bed stood the creature, almost eight feet in height, its terrible eyes staring at him. Its mouth opened as it tried to speak. Victor leapt from the bed, ran downstairs and hid in the courtyard, all the time dreading to meet the demon corpse to which he had given life.

When it was light the porter unlocked the courtyard gates and Frankenstein escaped into the streets of Ingolstadt. He walked and walked, hoping that the morning air would ease the heaviness of his mind. After some time he found himself outside the inn where the carriages stopped. Something made him pause. As he did so a familiar voice said, 'My dear Victor, how glad I am to see you. How lucky you should be passing here at the moment of my arrival.'

It was Henry Cherval. Victor was delighted. 'You don't know how happy I am to see you, Henry, but what are you doing here?'

'I persuaded my father to let me come to the university to study with you.' Then they talked of their families and friends.

'Your father, brothers and Elizabeth are well and very happy, Victor, although they wish you would write to them more often,' said Henry. 'But you look ill and pale, as if you have not been to bed for several nights.'

'Yes. You are right. I have been working hard for a long time on the same experiment and I have not had enough rest. That is finished now, I hope, so I promise to take more care.'

So saying, Frankenstein led his friend in the direction of his college. He trembled inwardly that the creature might still be in his apartments. The thought of seeing it again filled him with dread, but he feared even more that Henry might find out about it. When they reached the bottom of the stairs Victor said, 'Please wait here for a moment, Henry.' Then he went up alone. On the landing he pulled himself together a little but even so, shivered with fright. He threw the door open and stepped in. The apartment was empty. The hideous monster had gone. Victor was so relieved that he ran downstairs to Henry.

'Let us have breakfast,' he cried. But Victor was so excited he could not sit still, and he frequently got up and walked about the room laughing.

Henry became worried. 'My dear Victor, what is the matter?'

'Nothing,' replied Victor. Then suddenly he imagined that the monster had crept back into the room, and the shock of this fearful thought made him collapse.

* * *

After his collapse, Victor remained for several months in a lifeless state, suffering from a nervous fever. During all that time his friend Henry nursed him and watched over him.

Henry spared Victor's father and Elizabeth the worry of this by not letting them know how ill he

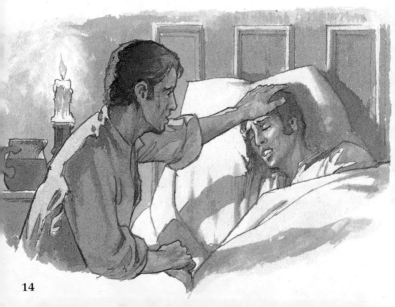

was. By spring, when the buds began to shoot on the trees outside his bedroom window, Victor was almost fully recovered.

'You are a good and kind friend, Henry, for you have spent all the winter nursing me. How shall I ever repay you?'

'First of all by writing to your father and Elizabeth. I have written many times but it would put their minds at rest to have a letter in your handwriting.'

The months passed and the two friends spent the summer in study.

The winter which followed was so severe that Victor's return home was delayed until May. It was almost three years since he had left Geneva. As he was preparing to leave he received a letter from his father. The news it contained made him weep with bitterness and grief.

One evening his father had taken a walk with
Elizabeth and Victor's two brothers. Little William
had run on and hidden himself in the trees. When
his elder brother Ernest went to look for him,
William was nowhere to be seen. As night came on,
Elizabeth and Victor's father fetched torches from
the house in Geneva, so that they could carry on
looking for the little boy. About five in the
morning, they found William's body. He had been
killed. On his neck were bruises from the
murderer's fingers.

Victor took the coach home immediately. When
he reached the mountains and the lake near his
home, he cried with joy. Later, as the night closed
round him, he began to feel the grip of grief and
fear. The city gates of Geneva were closed for the
night, and Victor had to go to a village close by. He

was unable to sleep, so he walked out to the place where William had been murdered. Before he reached there a storm blew up and the lightning soon flickered over the mountains and trees. It was a beautiful sight. The thunder crashed over his head. In one flash Victor saw a figure of gigantic size watching him. It was the monster!

In the next flash of lightning it was no longer there, but Frankenstein was now certain that the monster had killed little William. The thought sickened him.

He reached his home just after dawn, and Ernest met him. 'Father and Elizabeth are both ill with grief, Victor. Worse still, someone we all love has been arrested for the crime.'

Victor was stunned and unable to speak, for the accused person was Justine, a pretty, gentle girl who had lived with the Frankensteins for many years. She had nursed Victor's mother during her last illness, with great tenderness.

'Elizabeth says she will never believe it, whatever the evidence,' said Ernest.

'The poor girl is innocent,' agreed Victor. 'She must be released.'

'Her trial is today, Victor,' replied Ernest, 'and it looks bad for her. She was ill on the morning the body was found, and stayed in bed for several days. During that time a servant found a locket in Justine's clothes. Elizabeth had given it to William on the day he disappeared.'

'I tell you she is innocent,' repeated Victor.

His father was overjoyed to see him again after
such a long time, as was Elizabeth. She looked
more beautiful than ever. Despite her grief, she
showed Victor the greatest affection.

'Let us hope,' she said, 'that the judges do not
convict Justine. If they do, I shall be sad for ever.
We have lost darling William, but the innocent
must not be punished for it.'

Once the trial started, Victor lived in torment. He
could not speak out. Who would believe him? He
had not seen the killing, and he could not produce
the murderer. Justine looked calm but the
onlookers took this as a sign of lack of feeling, and
further proof of her guilt. Several witnesses were
called. There were two main pieces of evidence
against her. She had been seen near where the
body was found, and secondly, William's locket
containing a picture of his mother had been found
in her clothes afterwards.

Justine told the court that on the night of the murder she had visited her aunt who lived in a village outside Geneva. On her return at about nine o'clock, a man told her William was missing. She spent hours looking for him by which time the city gates of Geneva were shut and she could not go home. Until dawn she rested in a barn, sleeping in snatches.

'I walked near the place of William's death by chance,' she pleaded, 'and I have no idea how I got the locket.'

Several people who could have spoken well of Justine did not come forward, for they were frightened to be thought the friend of a murderess. Elizabeth had no such fears. She spoke for Justine in the crowded court, and told of the girl's fine character and of her gentleness and kindness. She reminded the listeners that Justine had nursed the late Madame Frankenstein with affection and care, and had loved little William as if he had been her own child.

'Justine would not have killed him for the picture,' said Elizabeth. 'She knows that we value her so much we would have given it to her.'

Although the people in the court were impressed by Elizabeth's generous appeal, they were not inclined to think that Justine was innocent. They thought only of her black ingratitude. When Victor saw the judges' faces, he rushed from the court in agony. He passed the night in wretched sleeplessness. At the court house, next morning, Justine was found guilty. On the following day she was executed.

*　　*　　*

Victor felt the pain of a tortured conscience, for it was his unholy experiment that had led to William and Justine losing their lives. He could not sleep, and his health was affected. His father misunderstood Victor's sadness. One day he said, 'You must not think only of William. We are all suffering, for we loved him, but it is our duty to think of the living.'

For a short time, Victor was strongly tempted to end his life. Then he thought of Elizabeth and his father and brother. How could he leave his dear ones unprotected against the creature?

In an attempt to forget, Victor went for a holiday
in the nearby Alpine valleys. The first part of the
journey he covered on horseback. Then as the way
became rugged and rough, he changed to the more
sure-footed mule.

It was mid-August and he enjoyed the mountains,
the rocks and the waterfalls. The higher he
climbed, the more magnificent was the sight. There
was snow on the mountains and the glaciers almost
reached the road. In the distance he heard the
rumbling of an avalanche.

At last Victor felt at peace, and that night he slept
soundly at a village inn. In the morning he felt so
calm and happy in his surroundings that he
decided to go higher. By noon he was looking
down on a wide expanse of ice.

   Suddenly he became aware of a huge thing, some
distance away, running towards him at an
astonishing speed. Victor began to tremble, for as
the shape approached he recognised the ugly
creature he had brought into the world.

   'You devil!' he shouted. 'How dare you come to
me after what you have done. The tortures of hell
are too mild for you!'

   'I am so miserable,' replied the demon. 'I am
hated and detested by all mankind. You made me,
and yet you want to kill me. If you will do what I
ask, I promise to leave you and your family in
peace. If you refuse I will destroy them all, one by
one.'

But Victor was full of rage and he hurled himself at the monster, who easily held him off.

'Be calm. You *must* hear my story,' pleaded the monster. 'Have I not suffered enough? Remember that you made me bigger and stronger than you are, and I am your creature. I will be mild and gentle if you perform what I ask. Everywhere there is goodness and happiness, but I am not allowed to share it. Make me happy, Frankenstein.'

'I will not. You are a wicked creature.'

'Please, Frankenstein. I am so alone. Everyone runs from me in disgust. The caves of ice and the wind and rain are kinder to me than mankind.'

'Cursed be the day I gave you life!'

'I do not want to be wicked, Frankenstein.'

'I do not want to be wretched,' replied Victor. 'But you have made me so, you detestable fiend.'

'Listen to my story, Frankenstein. And then it will rest with you whether I live a gentle life or ruin you all.'

After a pause Victor said, 'Very well. I will listen.'

They crossed the ice together and entered a hut. The creature lit a fire and then began his tale.

'When I ran away from your rooms in Ingolstadt that night long ago I was but newly made, and all my senses were confused. I could not understand light, or darkness, or heat, so I hid in the forest.'

'How did you keep alive?'

'I drank water from the brooks in the forest and I ate berries from the trees. I was cold and frightened in the dark and felt helpless and miserable. In the daytime it pleased me to listen to all the forest sounds, and especially the songs of the birds.'

'Did anyone see you?'

'Not at first. I knew there were people about because I found fire. Its warmth gave me joy, but when I put my fingers into the flame, it hurt me. I found out that I could eat nuts and roots as well as berries.'

'What made you leave the forest?'

'The search for food. I wandered for days. Soon the cold weather came on and it snowed. One day I saw a hut. The door was open, and I went in. An old man sat there. When he saw me he screamed and rushed out of the hut, across the fields.'

The creature told Frankenstein that he had
stayed in the warm hut and had eaten some bread,
cheese, milk and wine that had been left on the
table. 'I did not like the wine. Afterwards I walked
to a small village. I wanted to be friendly but the
children shrieked in fear, and one woman fainted
when she looked at me. The men threw stones at
me until I ran away, bruised and frightened. Some
distance away I found a disused hut, where I spent
the night.'

In the morning he had noticed a cottage close by
but did not show himself as he remembered his
treatment from the villagers the previous day. He
decided to hide in the hut for as long as he could.
To him it was a palace.

In the cottage lived an old man and his son and
daughter. The monster watched them through a
crack in the hut. They were unhappy, but
affectionate with one another.

'For the first time, Frankenstein, I saw gentleness and kindness and love. When the girl took an instrument and played it, I heard sweeter music than the birds could make. I was full of tears.'

Frankenstein looked at the creature. 'What is it you want me to do to make you happy?' he asked.

'Wait, Frankenstein. My story is not yet finished. They were graceful and beautiful to look at and so I wanted to join them but I dared not. Every day I listened to them and watched them. The old man was blind, and the two young ones were miserable because they were very poor. Sometimes they gave their father food even when they had none for themselves.'

'Why then did you leave such good people?'
asked Frankenstein.

'I did not want to, for I learned so much from
them. The whole winter passed and neither Agatha
the girl, nor Felix the boy, ever saw me.'

The monster explained that when they were
unhappy he too was unhappy, and when they were
full of joy, so was he. One day the creature saw his
own reflection in a pool of water, and he turned
away.

Often he saw Felix give some white flowers to his
sister and the monster wanted to do the same, but
he dared not. Sometimes during the nights
however he would bring firewood and food for
them. They were puzzled by this, but never found
out who had done it. The monster dreamed of the
little family, and felt they were superior beings.

Then one day an attractive young girl arrived on horseback. It seemed that her parents were dead and Felix and Agatha had befriended her in the

past. Felix was in love with her and called her his 'sweet Arabian'. It soon became clear to the monster that the Arabian, whose name was Safie, was trying to learn more of their language.

By listening to them talking together, the creature picked up more words, and when they were away he crept into their cottage to look at the books they used. He learned speedily, but the knowledge he gained made him sad.

'It made me realise, Frankenstein, that I was ignorant of my own creation and I had no friends, no relatives, no money and nothing of my own. All I had apart from great strength and some intelligence was a hideous face and an ugly shape. Where had I come from? I never had a father or mother. I had never been a child or had brothers or sisters. I had never been loved by anyone.'

Victor thought of his own happy childhood and looked at the monster for the first time with pity, but he did not speak.

'I had always been as I am, but until then I had known no evil.'

The monster gave Frankenstein a terrible look.

'It disgusted me to think how I had been made. I have cursed you for it, times without number.'

The creature fell silent for a few moments. Then he told how one day, when the father had been alone in the cottage, he had knocked on the door and entered. He had told the old man he was friendless and frightened, and that he would be an outcast for ever. The blind man was sympathetic, and they had begun to talk easily together.

Then without warning the door had opened and Felix had come in with Safie and Agatha. Immediately Safie rushed out, Agatha fainted and Felix dragged his father away. As the creature tried to put its arms round the old man, Felix had beaten him off with a stick.

'I ran into the wood and stayed there until night.
In the whole world there was no one who would
pity me and no one who would help me. I spent
the night in misery. A few days later I went back to
the cottage but it was empty. I never saw any of
them again.'

Sadly the creature turned its eyes on Victor.

'My thoughts turned to you, Frankenstein: my
creator. I knew you came from Geneva. The
journey here was long and hard, and I travelled at
night. Several times I lost my way. I felt full of
revenge.'

The creature's face softened a little.

'One day a little girl fell into a fast flowing river
near to where I was resting. I jumped into the
water and dragged her to the bank.'

All of a sudden the monster leapt to his feet and shouted, 'A man aimed a gun at me and put a bullet in my shoulder. Then he lifted the girl and carried her away. The wound took a long while to heal and all the time I thought of how I had been treated. I swore to take revenge on all mankind.'

'But why,' exclaimed Victor, 'should you attack my innocent brother, William?'

'It was not like that at all. I was resting one evening outside Geneva when a child came running near. The moment he saw me he screamed and covered his eyes. I told him I would not hurt him, but he called me wretch and ogre and said he would tell his papa Frankenstein, the magistrate, to punish me.'

'And you killed a little boy!'

'I did not intend to. He called me dreadful names so I put my hands on his throat to silence him. In a moment he was dead.'

'An innocent girl has been executed for that!' shouted Victor.

'I took a locket from his neck. It held the picture of a lady.'

'What did you do with it?'

'Something wicked. I found a barn to hide in but a young woman was asleep on some straw. The fiend inside me told me to make her pay for my murder so I put the locket in her dress. Then I wandered here. Now my story is finished.'

'When you began it,' said Victor, 'you said there was something I could do to make you happy.'

'Yes, I am alone and miserable. You must create another being: a woman as deformed and ugly as I am, who will live with me and love me and be my wife. Only you can do it.'

'I refuse. Never again will I create wickedness.'

'You are wrong, Frankenstein,' replied the fiend. 'I would live in kindness with people but they will not let me. If I cannot have love I will cause fear.'

His face wrinkled in agony.

'Make a creature who loves me, who does not run from me, and I will make peace with you. Make me happy. Do not deny me! We will go away together and you will never see us again. I swear it. Please!'

Victor was upset by the creature's distress and after a long pause he said quietly, 'I consent. I will make you a mate.'

'Go then, Frankenstein, and begin your work.'

So saying, the monster departed before Victor could reply or change his mind.

*   *   *

Victor sat for some time before making his way down towards the valley. Darkness fell. At the half-way resting place he sat down next to the fountain. He wept bitterly as he thought of what he had promised. By dawn he had reached the village, and from there he went home to his family.

Try as he would Victor could not bring himself to start work on another creation, although he feared the anger of the fiend. His mind was also taken up with his forthcoming marriage to Elizabeth.

'I am so happy, Victor,' said his father. 'When shall it be?'

Victor did not reply immediately. The thought of marrying Elizabeth while the monster still threatened him, filled him with horror. He knew that he would have to give the monster a mate first, and he could not set up a laboratory in the house for fear of discovery. His father had tried many times however to persuade him to take a long holiday to restore his health completely, and now he agreed.

It was decided that Victor should go to England for at least six months, then marry Elizabeth upon his return to Geneva. Henry Cherval was to accompany him. Although it worried Victor that he was leaving his family and future bride open to attack from the monster, he remembered that the creature had said that he would follow Frankenstein wherever he went.

In September Victor packed as many of his chemical instruments as he could. Then he and Henry made their way by coach across Europe. From Rotterdam they crossed the sea to Dover.

In England, Victor began to collect the materials necessary for his new creation. The weeks passed, then they received an invitation to visit Scotland. This was Victor's opportunity, because he was very behind with his work. He told Henry he wanted to be alone in Scotland for a time, to recover his spirits. He went to a desolate and remote island off the Scottish coast and tried to begin his work. There were just five other people on the island.

The task sickened him and he grew restless and nervous, dreading that the monster might appear.

Suppose this female became more violent than her mate? Suppose they disliked one another? Suppose she did not agree to go away and leave Frankenstein? Suppose they had children who themselves were monsters? All these questions weighed on his mind.

One evening as he worked he looked up and saw the demon watching him through the window, a dreadful smile on its face. All of a sudden

Frankenstein realised what he was doing and in a
fit of passion he tore the thing he had been making
to pieces.

Outside the window the monster howled. 'After I
have waited so long, you have destroyed what you
promised me. You are my creator, Frankenstein,
but I am your master now. I will be revenged.
Remember me, Frankenstein, I shall be with you
on your wedding night!'

After he had gone, Victor's mind was in a whirl.
The monster's words kept swirling round in his
head. 'I shall be with you on your wedding night.'
The night passed. Frankenstein could not sleep.

In the morning a fisherman brought him a
packet of letters. One was from Henry Cherval,
who suggested that Victor should join him. This
Victor decided to do.

First however he went into his laboratory and
put the remains of the half-finished creature into a
large basket. Just after midnight he took a small
boat and when he was about four miles from
shore, dropped the basket, which he had weighted
with heavy stones, into the sea.

Two days later he reached the town where Henry
was staying and made his way to his friend's
lodgings. He was too late! The fiend had got there
before him. Henry was dead, with the mark of the
monster's fingers on his neck. Victor looked on the
lifeless form of his friend; he shook violently and
collapsed in a fever.

When they found him beside the body he was suspected of being the murderer and a charge was prepared. For two months he stayed in his prison cell, raving like a madman. The magistrate tried to question him, without success.

As he regained his health, Victor thought often of Justine, executed in innocence. Maybe he would suffer the same penalty. Then one day the magistrate returned.

'When you first became ill,' he explained, 'I examined the papers from your pocket and so was able to trace your family. I wrote to Geneva nearly two months ago. We know now that you were a close friend of Mr Cherval and the shock of his murder made you ill again. Your father has arrived here and wishes to take you home.'

The first words Victor said were, 'Are Elizabeth and Ernest well protected?' His father calmed him, saying that they were both safe.

The court dismissed the case against Victor and he left prison with his father. On the way home his father tried to make him more cheerful by talking about the forthcoming marriage to Elizabeth. All Victor could think of was watching over his loved ones until he could destroy the monster for ever.

One day on the journey home he told his father that he had been the cause of the death of William, Justine and Henry, but his father would not hear of it.

'My dear son, please don't say that again,' he said softly.

So Victor remained silent, but the words of the monster came back to him. 'I shall be with you on your wedding night.' He was convinced that on that night the creature would try to kill him.

Elizabeth's eyes filled with tears when she saw how thin and frail he was. She was as sweet and gentle as she had always been. Victor wanted desperately to marry her. In the meantime, while preparations went ahead for the wedding, he took care to have loaded pistols and a dagger always within reach.

It was decided that the couple should spend their honeymoon at a villa beside the lake where Elizabeth's parents had lived. After the ceremony the newly-married pair left by lake from Geneva, planning to stay that night at Evian. They landed at eight in the evening. Before returning to the inn

they walked along the shore, but the words of the
monster would not stay out of Victor's mind.

'I shall be with you on your wedding night.'

He was so agitated that, when Elizabeth went to
their room, he felt he had to find out where the
monster was. First he walked through the passage
of the inn, expecting to see the creature at every
turn. As he did so, he heard a dreadful scream
from Elizabeth.

Victor rushed into their room, but he was too
late. His bride was lying across the bed, lifeless,
with the mark of the fiend's grasp on her neck.
Looking through the unshuttered window was the
hideous murderer. He pointed his finger at the
body of Elizabeth, and laughed.

Frankenstein ran to the window and fired his
pistol, but the creature moved with the swiftness of
light, and plunged into the lake. The noise of the
pistol shot brought a crowd into the room. When
Victor pointed to the lake, they took to the boats
and followed the murderer's track. But it was in
vain. After several hours they returned.

Frankenstein collapsed from exhaustion and was put to bed. The full horror of all that had happened grew in his mind. The killing of William, the execution of Justine, the murder of Henry, and now his own wife. The idea that his father and his brother Ernest were in danger made Victor shudder – and then act.

He returned at once to Geneva. The news of what had happened broke Victor's father, for he had loved Elizabeth as his own child. A few days later he died in Victor's arms.

In his despair, Victor formed a plan to pursue his monster until he could destroy it. Before leaving Geneva he paid his last visit to the cemetery where the bodies of William, Elizabeth and his father rested. It was getting dark as he knelt on the grass and prayed aloud for help to find and kill the cursed monster.

As if in answer, out of the stillness, came a loud and wicked laugh. Then the creature said softly. 'I am satisfied, Frankenstein, now that you are miserable and wretched.' With that, he disappeared at great speed.

For months Victor trailed him, guided by small clues, but he could never catch up with him. He traced him along the windings of the river shore, and followed him close along parts of the Mediterranean coastline.

Through country after country the demon kept a day ahead of Victor, then by ship across the Black Sea, then amidst the wilds of Tartary and the wastes of Russia. All the time it avoided populated places.

Each time Victor lost trace of him, the fiend would return and leave some mark. He was enjoying the torment he gave. Victor had no peace except when he was asleep. But by day, the thought of revenge kept him going.

One night he heard a voice in the darkness. 'You must follow me now to the bitter cold and ice of the north. There you will have more hard and miserable hours to endure before I am satisfied that you have suffered enough, my enemy.'

On Victor went. Then, when the cold was almost too severe to bear, he saw a speck in the distance. Just when it seemed he had caught up with his foe, the wind arose, the sea roared, the ice cracked and split. He was left drifting on a shattered piece of ice.

Many frightening hours passed. The ice came to rest but Victor could not go on. His mind was filled with thoughts of William, Justine, Henry, Elizabeth and his father. He thought of his own life and how he had thrown his talents aside. His strength ebbed away. He was totally exhausted. He lay on the ice and closed his eyes.

The next day the monster, realising he was no longer being tracked, returned to look for his maker. When he saw Victor's frozen body, in the falling darkness, he was almost moved to tears.

'Forgive me, Frankenstein. I destroyed everything you loved. But I have suffered great misery myself. You cannot hear me say this, but I did not want to kill them. It is all ended now. You are my last victim.' So saying the creature bowed his head in wretchedness.

'Why did Felix drive me from the cottage? Why did the peasant shoot me when I saved his child? Is that why I have murdered the lovely and the helpless? Now you are dead, Frankenstein. What is there left for me, but death?'

The monster turned and disappeared into the darkness.

Stories . . . that have stood the test of time

SERIES 740
FABLES
A first book of Aesop's Fables
A second book of Aesop's Fables
Aladdin and his wonderful lamp
Ali Baba and the forty thieves
Famous Legends (Book 1)
Famous Legends (Book 2)
La Fontaine's Fables:
The Fox turned Wolf
Folk Tales from around the World

SERIES SL – LARGE FORMAT
Aesop's Fables
Gulliver's Travels

Ladybird titles cover a wide range of subjects and reading ages.
Write for a free illustrated list from the publishers:
LADYBIRD BOOKS LTD Loughborough Leicestershire England